MILLY AND THE MACY'S PARADE

1924

BY SHANA COREY ★ ILLUSTRATED BY BRETT HELQUIST

SCHOLASTIC INC.

NEW YORK TORONTO LONDON AUCKLAND
SYDNEY MEXICO CITY NEW DELHI HONG KONG

THE AUTHOR AND THE ARTIST GRATEFULLY ACKNOWLEDGE:

THE WONDERFUL PEOPLE AT MACY'S: ROBIN HALL, DIANA ROIO, AND

BOB RUTAN FOR THEIR TIME, ENTHUSIASM, AND SUPPORT OF THIS BOOK; AND, MOST ESPECIALLY,

RACHELLE STERN FOR HER INVALUABLE KNOWLEDGE OF MACY'S HISTORY, HER UNFAILING HUMOR AND INSIGHT

(AND HER WILLINGNESS TO SHARE THEM), AND FOR THE TWO FASCINATING AND FUN BEHIND-THE-SCENES TOURS SHE GAVE US.

THE ALWAYS PLEASANT AND PATIENT LIBRARIANS AT BROOKLYN'S CENTRAL LIBRARY FOR THEIR HELP WITH FINDING *THE NEW YORK TIMES* MICROFILM FROM THE 1920S.

THE EXTENSIVE RESOURCES OF THE INTERNET; IN PARTICULAR, NYCTOURIST.COM FOR INTRODUCING US TO THE PARADE'S HISTORY AND INSPIRING THIS STORY. THE TALENTED TEAM AT SCHOLASTIC PRESS WHOSE HARD

WORK AND CREATIVITY MADE THIS BOOK POSSIBLE: TRACY MACK, EDITOR EXTRAORDINAIRE; MARIJKA KOSTIW, THE WORLD'S MOST AMAZING ART DIRECTOR; AND LESLIE BUDNICK, HANDLER OF ALL THINGS GREAT AND SMALL.

AND, ABOVE ALL, ALL OF AMERICA'S IMMIGRANTS, WHO BRAVELY COME TO THIS COUNTRY AND ENRICH IT WITH THEIR CULTURES AND TRADITIONS.

FOR MY GRANDMOTHERS
PAULINE KLEIN ZACKS (1918–2001)
AND RUTH KIRSCH COREY
WITH LOVE —S.C.

FOR ADELINE
—B.H.

It was 1924, Milly's first year in America, and all over New York City people were hustling and bustling about getting ready for the holidays.

At the center of all the hubbub was Macy's, the great department store where Milly's papa worked. And watching it all from his private penthouse office was Mr. Macy.

Papa said Mr. Macy was just about the most important person in America (next to the president of course), and Milly was inclined to agree. She visited Mr. Macy's store every day after school. It was like a giant present waiting to be unwrapped!

Woosh!
She went
around and
around
in the
revolving doors.
Up, up, up
she sailed on the
great escalator.
Down,
down,
down
she rode in the
grand elevator.

She flew from
fashions to
home furnishings.
She breezed
through ball gowns,
swirled
through scarves,
loitered
in ladies lingerie,
and she always,
always
tried out all the toys.
Milly thought
Macy's was magic.

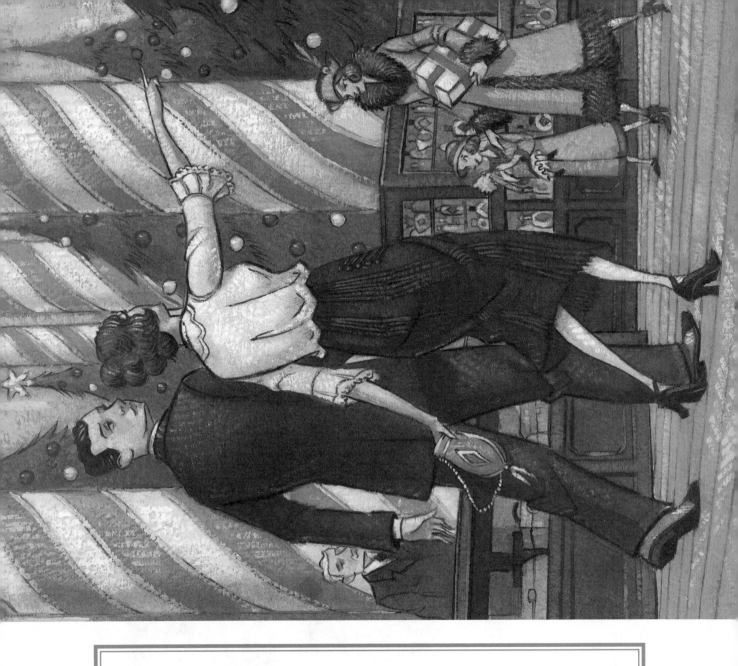

And Milly wasn't the
only one. Thousands
of people streamed into
the store every day. Most
of them took one look
at the trinkets and the
treasures, the glamour
and the glitter, and
said the same thing:
Gorgeous.

But some of them did not.

Some of them only pressed their noses against the windows and sighed. "It's not like home," they said.

Milly remembered what it was like to be homesick. When her family first came to America from Poland, they had been homesick, too. Mama had missed Polish foods. Papa had missed Polish words. And Milly had missed just about everything.

But after many months, Milly's family was starting to get used to America.

Mama was finding places to buy Polish foods (and sometimes trying American foods!).

Papa was learning new American words.

And at Macy's, Milly was pretending to be a princess—and making all sorts of American friends in the process.

Still, being homesick was a horrible feeling. And no one should be homesick during the holidays. Milly went out to the delivery dock to talk to Papa about it. She found him resting, with a faraway look in his eyes.

"What's wrong?" asked Milly.

"I miss our holidays back home," said Papa. "I love America, but everything here feels different."

"I miss home, too," said Papa's friend Herman. "In my country, I was surrounded by friends and family. How can I celebrate when I'm all alone?"

"Nothing in America is the same as it was in the old country," agreed Albert. "In my country, we celebrate with big brass instruments and caroling from house to house."

"It would take a hundred years to go caroling to all the apartments in New York City," sighed Papa. "Maybe we won't ever have a real holiday celebration in America."

Milly looked from one sad drooping face to the other.

And that was when she had her idea. The most marvelous idea that ever a little girl had.

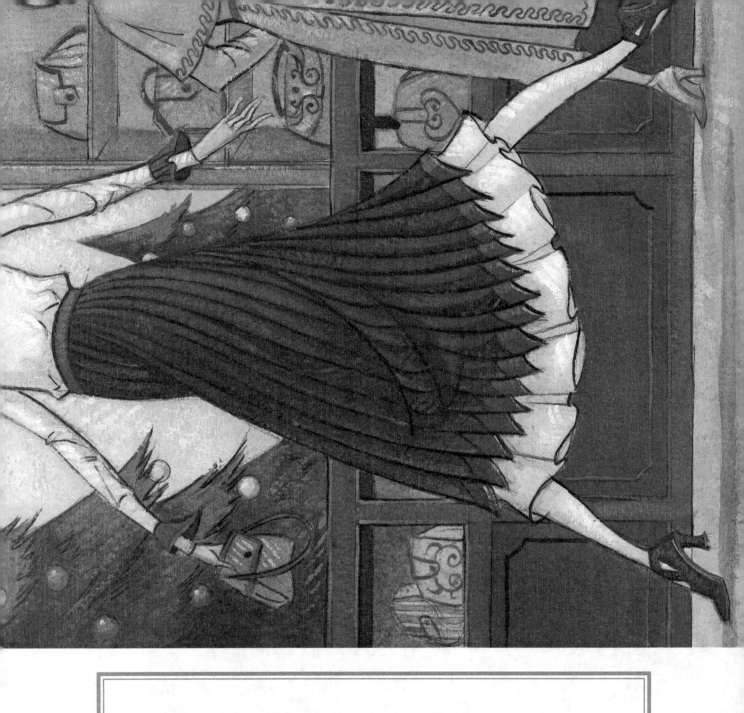

There was only one person who could bring that kind of holiday celebration to America.

Milly raced back into the store, past the perfumes and the purses, the diamonds and the dolls, all the way up to the thirteenth floor.

At the top of the escalator was his door. Milly pushed it open a crack.

Inside his office, Mr. Macy was pacing back and forth. "Why it's almost Thanksgiving, and Christmas is right around the corner," he grumbled. "But the salesclerks are all frowning when they should be festive. It's depressing the customers!"

Mr. Macy's assistant, Mr. Snidely, snickered. "Maybe we should fire them."

Fire them? Fire Papa and his friends?

"No!" Milly cried. "You can't fire them!"

"What?" thundered Mr. Macy. "Who said that?"

Milly stepped forward. "Um . . . I did sir, I didn't mean to be rude. It's just that, I don't think firing people will make them any more festive."

"What are you doing here, little girl?" asked Mr. Snidely.

Milly gulped. Then she told Mr. Macy and Mr. Snidely all about Papa and his friends and their holiday celebrations back home.

"Hmmmm," said Mr. Macy. "Homesick, you don't say. I've been homesick myself before. But still, how can we cure homesickness?"

Milly explained her plan. Maybe, just maybe, Macy's could bring a little bit of everyone's home to America.

"What?" asked Mr. Macy. "Singing and strolling in the streets?"

"Ridiculous," scoffed Mr. Snidely. "No one will come."

But Mr. Macy didn't seem to hear him. There was a twinkle in his eyes that hadn't been there before. "I like the way you think," he said to Milly.

The next day, there was a sign posted at Macy's.

"A parade," said Papa, "with singing and strolling in the streets?"

"Yes!" said Milly. "Just like in the old country."

Soon word began to spread.

"Say kid," whispered Flossie at the Follies. "Didya hear about the parade on Thanksgiving?"

"Gee whiz, it sounds swell!" Trixie answered between kicks.

"What's this about a holiday parade?" asked Mr. Rockefeller at breakfast. "Should we buy it for the children?"

"I don't think the parade is for sale, dear," replied his wife. "But if the Vanderbilts are going, we'd better go, too."

On the morning of the
parade, Milly and Papa
woke up extra early. They
dressed in costumes that
Mama had made for
them.

"I'll be watching from
the sidewalk," she said as
she waved good-bye.

Then Milly and Papa
took the elevated train
all the way uptown to
Harlem where everyone
was meeting.

When they got there, the streets were filled with people.

All the Macy's workers were dressed up and ready to march.

"Let's have a parade!" shouted Mr. Macy.

All at once, cowboys and clowns, knights and sheikhs began marching down the street. A band played a polka. Papa and his friends sang and strolled just as they had in the old country.

In the middle of it all, Milly rode on an elephant borrowed from the Central Park Zoo.

"That's my daughter," said Mama proudly as Milly passed by.

"Lovely," murmured Mrs. Rockefeller.

"Now *this* is a celebration!" called Papa over the roar of the crowd.

"Yes!" said Papa's friend Herman. "An American celebration!"

Everyone agreed that the parade was a huge success.

"Maybe we should do this every year," Milly suggested.

"Well," began Mr. Snidely, "I hardly think . . ."

Mr. Macy gave him a sharp look.

"Yes, Milly," finished Mr. Snidely meekly. "Marvelous idea, Milly."

And that's how Milly and Mr. Macy started a new holiday tradition. It looked a little like the old country, and a little like America, and a little like something entirely new.

Who would have thought that one marvelous idea could give so many different people something to celebrate together?

COME ONE COME ALL
to the
MACY'S CHRISTMAS PARADE
SEE THE ANIMALS FROM THE CENTRAL PARK ZOO!

AUTHOR'S NOTE

This is a true story—partly. Milly is a made-up character and the parts about Milly and her family are fiction, as are the depictions of all the characters in the book. In fact, the real Mr. Macy died in 1877, long before the first Macy's Parade. But he was immortalized in the 1947 classic book and film *Miracle on 34th Street*, and to this day, the store continues to get letters addressed to him. Because so many Americans associate his name with the store and the parade, I chose to use him as the face of Macy's in this story, as well. (After all, there couldn't very well be a Macy's Parade without a Mr. Macy!)

The parade itself is, of course, real. It has been an American tradition for 78 years and counting, and today millions of people tune in to the parade on television or watch it from the parade route in New York City.

The tradition wasn't always a part of American culture, though. In fact, it comes from a combination of other cultures. It originated in 1924 with immigrants who worked at Macy's and missed the holiday traditions of their homelands. When all those immigrants got together, cultures blended and they created something uniquely American.

More than a thousand Macy's employees marched in that first parade. Joining them were bands, floats (like the one pictured in the photograph below), and 25 animals from the Central Park Zoo. The parade started at 145th Street and ended five miles later in front of Macy's department store on 34th Street, where Santa Claus was officially welcomed to New York City. A quarter of a million people lined the parade route to watch. The parade was met with so much enthusiasm, that the very next day Macy's announced that it would become an annual event.

Although it has always been held on Thanksgiving Day, that first year, the parade was called the Macy's Christmas Parade. But in later years it became known as the Macy's Thanksgiving Day Parade, a tradition that embraces people of all faiths and cultures and brings them together to kick off the holiday season.

The first balloon appeared in the parade in 1927. In the early years, the balloons were released at the end of the parade. The giant characters would float for days, and whoever finally found them could claim a prize.

In all its years, the parade has missed only three holidays. From 1942–1944 it was canceled because of World War II. All the rubber balloons were donated to be used as scrap rubber for the war effort. The parade resumed in 1945 and has been ringing in the holidays ever since.

No one knows exactly whose idea it was first, but maybe, just maybe, it started with a little girl like Milly . . . a little girl with a marvelous idea.